KEEPER OF THE COMPASS:

SECRETS

Written by Debbie K. Thomas
Illustrated by Aprylle Magar

FERNE PRESS

Keeper of the Compass: Secrets

Copyright © 2012 by Debbie K. Thomas

Illustrations by Aprylle Magar
Illustrations created with pencil
Layout and cover design by Susan Leonard

Printed in the United States.

Summary: While in Hawaii, a young girl discovers her true path.

Library of Congress Cataloging-in-Publication Data
Thomas, Debbie K.
Keeper of the Compass: Secrets/Debbie K. Thomas–First Edition
ISBN-13: 978-1-938326-02-8
1. Juvenile Fiction. 2. Hawaii. 3. Divorce. 4. Self-confidence.
5. Self-discovery.
I. Thomas, Debbie K. II. Title
Library of Congress Control Number: 2012940405

FERNE PRESS

Ferne Press is an imprint of Nelson Publishing & Marketing
366 Welch Road, Northville, MI 48167
www.nelsonpublishingandmarketing.com
(248) 735-0418

This book is dedicated to my fifth grade students, at Doherty Elementary, who were my first audience, and to all my past students for their inspiration. May all the children who read this book let their internal compass keep them on the right path.

I would like to acknowledge my husband, Craig, and children, Dana and Kirk, for their unwavering encouragement throughout this journey. I would also like to thank my sister, Cindy Yantis, for her inspiration and advice. My parents, John and Jane Yantis, were instrumental in teaching me to follow my internal compass and to persevere as I set new goals for myself throughout my life. I'd like to thank my illustrator, Aprylle Magar, for bringing my story to life with her beautiful illustrations. Thank you goes to my editor and project manager, Kris Yankee, for her suggestions. I would also like to thank my publisher, Marian Nelson, for seeing the potential in my seed idea and for her positive energy.

CHAPTER 1

THE BIG FIND

My stomach flipped as I gripped the edge of my seat a little harder. The airplane suddenly hit a rough spot. Attached to the seat ahead of me was my meal tray with my Coke slopping from side to side. Some managed to spill out of the cup, quickly making its way off the edge of the tray and onto my drawing pad, which sat on my lap. Just then I heard the pilot announce, "Please keep your seatbelt fastened. We are currently experiencing a bumpy patch as we descend to the Honolulu airport."

Looking down the aisle, I could see my bratty little nine-year-old brother, Timmy, stretching his arms, yawning, and looking like a rug rat with his messy mop of bedhead. He didn't seem to be bothered by the bumpy flight. At least we didn't have to sit together, I thought.

Today I was eleven years, one month, and thirteen days old. My life would never be what I once knew it to be. My brother and I were traveling across the country by ourselves for the first time without a parent.

1

I peered out the window to see the miniature roads and cars below. It looked like Timmy's tiny village collection that my dad had happily passed down to him from when he was a kid. The houses and buildings looked like toys that could easily be tossed aside.

The plane began to tip sideways, directing the window I was looking through up to the clouds. Whiteness filled the window as we continued through more clouds. Finally we began to approach the runway and my stomach did another turn. The plane leveled out and the flight attendant quickly collected all the drink cups. I folded the tabletop back up into the seat ahead and prepared for landing.

It was so loud as we began to descend! I had to cover my ears. I chewed harder on a piece of Juicy Fruit gum from the pack my dad had given me. He told me it would help to pop my ears as we went down. I braced myself for the landing, not sure what to expect. I closed my eyes until I could feel the plane hit the ground. The plane bounced a little as the wheels hit the runway. Phew! We made it!

We gathered our bags from the overhead bins. I had my red rolling suitcase with my nametag neatly attached. Timmy had his royal blue rolling suitcase with a very worn stuffed dog attached, which he had fondly named Bailey after our pet dog that had died two years earlier. Timmy never left that thing behind. He kept it closer than ever now that we were going through The Change.

As we juggled our stuff down the airplane steps, I saw a familiar face in the distance. Mom stood by the gate with the biggest grin I'd ever seen. She was tan and her hair more blonde than usual. She actually looked more rested and happier than I'd seen her in a long time. Her long white walking shorts and bright yellow flowered halter top showed off her tan and her white teeth even more. I noticed she was holding something colorful in her hand.

When we finally reached her, all I could hear was "Aloha!" as she draped the flowered necklace around each of our necks and kissed us on the cheeks.

"This is a Hawaiian tradition," Mom explained, "when people show their admiration by presenting a flowered lei."

It smelled so fresh and fragrant! After that long airplane ride, it felt good to cover up that smelly B.O. with the beautiful scent of Hawaiian flowers.

Although I had butterflies in my stomach about seeing this new place I had never dreamed of visiting, I had to keep tough and not let Mom see me soften up. After all, it was her fault I was here, so far away from my dad and friends.

"Well, how was your flight?" asked Mom.

"Long and bumpy," I snapped.

"What about you, little guy?" she asked as she ruffled Timmy's already messy hair.

"It was okay. I met this fat woman next to me that ended up being really nice. She had candy, and we talked about her dog and I told her all about Bailey. I told her about the time that..."

My mind wandered as Timmy continued to babble all the way through the airport. I noticed groups and groups of people all happily chatting, hugging, and smiling with their tan faces and white teeth. Then I looked down, noticing the white chalky skin on my arms. I will never fit in here. I will never be that tan. And I will never be that happy again!

The three of us walked across the open-air airport until we saw the bright red AIR KAUAI sign hanging in the distance. Mom pointed to the helicopter. We followed the arrow until we spotted the large red helicopter parked on the helipad ready for takeoff.

"We're not there yet?" I questioned.

"Almost! We are going on the helicopter for the last leg of the trip to the island of Kauai," Mom explained. "It's one of the six main islands that make up the state of Hawaii."

We ran to the helicopter, hugging our things to us as the strong wind of the propellers almost blew us away. I ducked my head as I climbed aboard and squeezed into the small helicopter that only held four seats. Hearing the loud roar of the engine, I couldn't help but feel a little scared and excited at the same time.

When the helicopter approached the round-shaped island of Kauai, the mountains were like a perfect painting. I got chills when we came up over the island for the first time. The rugged landscape met the turquoise water of the ocean. No one could describe the grandeur of them. The mountains were massive emerald green with rusty red rock throughout. We wore headphones to protect our ears from the loudness of the helicopter. It was cool that the pilot could talk to us through the headphones, and there was even background music!

The pilot explained in his soothing voice, "Forty-five percent of this island is natural with no inhabitants."

I looked out the window in awe. These mountains are awesome, I thought as the helicopter dipped into the valley. Whoa! My stomach did a flip. I thought this was a helicopter, not a roller coaster!

"Look at those!" I said as I pointed at the many beautiful waterfalls cascading down the mountainside surrounded by tropical plant life.

Just then the pilot pointed and continued, "That's the Makauwahi (ma-cow-wah-he) Sinkhole, the largest limestone cave complex in the Hawaiian Islands. It's the current site in which archaeologists from all over the world are learning about Hawaii's history, with a record of life that dates back ten thousand years."

My mom couldn't stop vigorously nodding her head and gesturing toward the site where she'd already been working for the past month. The helicopter landed at a small airport on a field between two mountains. Mom's car was parked close by.

The ride from the small valley airport in Mom's little yellow compact car seemed like forever even though it was only a thirty-five-minute drive. It was quiet with the occasional, "Oh, that's cool!" from Timmy. I stared out the window with no comment or expression. The tall buildings of the city were a distant memory. Now we were on a winding road that was close enough to the edge of the island to see the Pacific Ocean. I had never been to the ocean. Wow! The waves were massive here! It reminded me of Lake Michigan, which you couldn't see across, but it was definitely a different color. Lake Michigan was more of a brown or dark, dark blue depending on the season. The ocean was a beautiful crystal-clear aquamarine, just like the colored pencil I had in my bag.

Mom turned down a narrow road, and we continued to wind and wind and wind another couple of miles until we came to the end. All I could see were six small tents and one rather large tent set up to the side. There were sticks with string tying each stick together arranged in a big square with lots of little squares in between. There were flags at the end of each row with different letters and numbers organized in some way. It reminded me of the map grids we learned about in geography with Mrs. Fuller.

"What are we doing here?" I asked. The only thing I wanted to do was get to the house where we were going to be staying, get out my drawing pad, and begin to draw.

"Well," Mom said with a broad smile, "I wanted to show you where I've been working for the past month. And I need to have a quick meeting with Mr. Flannigan, the archaeological chairman."

"What does quick meeting mean?" I asked with an edge to my voice.

"You can take Timmy to that tent over there and see some of the ancient artifacts that have been found so far. I should be done by the time you're finished investigating."

"Oh cool!" Timmy yelled as he ran toward the orange tent that Mom had pointed out. This is what I hate about being the BIG sister. I always have to be the responsible one and get stuck watching the Brat. That's the way it has always been, though. I guess some things never change, no matter where we live.

I walked carefully over the uneven ground and noticed piles of dirt inside some of the squares on the grid. There were a few people scattered throughout the grid, each in their own square. It almost looked like little moles working on building tunnels or bumblebees working busily in their own little cell of the hive. I continued across the valley to the tent that Timmy had already gone into.

By the time I got there, Timmy was already interviewing a lady who was working in the tent.

"Hi. You must be Tori," the lady said. "I'm Gretta Greenfield. Just call me Gretta."

"Hi," I said as I noticed all the dirty, rusty items sitting on a tarp on the ground.

"Come in and look around. I just was showing Timmy some of our recent treasures. You'll notice tags on each with a letter and number that corresponds to where they were found at the dig site. We identify rows by letters and each column with numbers. Then we know exactly where each item was found," explained Gretta.

I walked around and saw that everything looked old and dirty. They were surely going to clean this junk up before turning them in to the museum. I bent down closer to the ground so I could inspect each item. I spotted a clouded mirror with a tag that said H32. There was part of what looked like a clay pot with a tag M42. Then I saw something that looked like it could have been an arrowhead like those I saw at the Chippewa Indian Reservation in Michigan. It appeared to be carved from stone.

As I was turning to see what Timmy was doing, *flash*, a sparkle caught the corner of my eye. It came from the other side of the tarp. I slowly moved closer. *flash*! What was that? It was coming from a pile of things all with the tag T11. I touched the dirty pile of I-don't-know-what to see if anything was sparkling. I could feel something warm. I picked it up to inspect it closer. Not sure what it was, I had an irresistible urge to slip it into my pocket. So…I did.

CHAPTER 2

SHE DOESN'T KNOW ANYTHING

I couldn't wait to get out of there. I could feel the warmth of what was inside my pocket, and I knew it was wrong. But it was too late now! I had made the decision that whatever it was wouldn't be missed. There were too many other things that seemed much more important than this. Then I heard, "Tori, Timmy, let's go!" from outside the tent. Phew!

Mom drove around the mountainside on another curvy road like the one before. At the end of the road was a small house nestled next to a mountain. Well, in some places it may be considered a house, but to me it looked more like a shack. It was a small, square structure made of wood, sitting on stilts that raised it about five feet above the ground. The peeling green paint accented the rusty roof, which was made of some sort of bumpy metal. The front porch was slightly lopsided but had an inviting wooden rocking chair to the left of the door just like on my grandma's porch.

This is what we were to call home for the next six months. I couldn't help but think of the contrast between this shack and our big, beautiful home with Dad back in Northville, Michigan. People would say we lived a very comfortable life when we were a whole family unit. Now the big house in Northville seemed empty of laughter and adventure, but at least it had all the conveniences most any kid would want. People would always say, "The Chapmans have the dream house." We had the best movie room with the largest big-screen TV of any of our friends. We had every Wii and Xbox game and a huge movie collection, as well as foosball, ping pong, and pool tables, and the old-fashioned pinball machine that sat in the corner. I have to admit it was a preteen's paradise.

"This is it! Isn't it wonderful?" Mom sang out with her irritatingly optimistic attitude.

"I wouldn't exactly call it wonderful," I added my two cents.

"I love it!" shouted Timmy as he spotted the rugged rocky backdrop of the house. He ran past the house, dropped his bag, and immediately found the first stepping stone that would hold his weight. He began to shimmy up the steep incline to begin his first exploration.

All I could do was shake my head in disgust and begin rolling my suitcase toward the porch.

"Tori, I know you aren't happy with the arrangements, but it will only be six months. Look at it as an adventure!" Mom pleaded.

"An adventure? Everything's an adventure to you. This is more like prison! You make me leave my home, my friends, and Dad!" I cried.

"Tori, I love you and Dad loves you, but we just don't love each other anymore. You have to understand how hard it is to have to share you and Timmy with him."

"Blah blah blah!" I blurted as I dropped my suitcase, covered my ears with my hands, and ran into the house.

I couldn't take this anymore. With my ears covered and my eyes closed, I thought maybe I could shut this out a little longer. I didn't want to hear one more time that the divorce wasn't my fault. Of course it was my fault! At least maybe a little bit.

By the time Mom made it into the house with the suitcases, I had already found my way to the extra bedroom. OMG! There are two beds in here! That could only mean one thing, I realized. "I'm going to have to SHARE A ROOM with the RUG RAT!" I screamed.

Throwing myself onto the bed, I began to sob. Things just seemed to be getting worse. I thought about my best friend at home, Bella. I needed her more than ever. Whenever Bella or I had problems at home, we would immediately text on our phones or chat on the computer in Facebook or Skype. Now she was so far away!

Wait a minute, I realized, it doesn't matter the distance. We can Skype or text anywhere!

Carefully I opened my yellow backpack that was stuffed to the brim with items I thought I needed on the plane. I took out my iPod, colored pencils and drawing pad, *Teen* magazine, and the bag of Skittles Dad had given me for the plane and lined them up neatly on my bed. Then I could easily reach my MacBook that I had gotten for Christmas.

The laptop was cool to the touch, which was unusual because it normally felt warm with all the use it would get throughout the day. Now the computer was the only connection I had to back home and my real life. Maybe Mom could take away Dad, take away my home, take away my friends, but she would never take away my computer.

Once the computer was all booted up, I logged into Facebook. Thank God I could get on! I immediately posted a new status: HAWAII SUCKS!!!

After checking out the statuses of a few friends, I noticed that Bella was online even though the five-hour time difference made it midnight back in Michigan. I began typing on the private chat room on Facebook.

T: Hey Bella what's up

B: Hi Tori how wuz ur trip?

T: What do u think w/ the brat bro tagging along?

B: Oh yeah that can get irritating

T: I wanna come home!!!!!!!

B: why? u just got there.

T: It's boring & you wouldn't believe who I have
2 share a room with!

B: No way! ur mom put Timmy the booger biter
in w/u?

T: Yeah it's not a pretty situation ;-(

B: Ouch! that sucks! I'm sry

T: Thanx

B: TTYL-g2g-dad's coming!

With that, Bella logged off.

Then I felt the warmth of what sat in the safety of my pocket. I carefully pulled it out and noticed the glass front of what looked like a clock. I didn't see numbers or letters under the dirt-covered glass. I decided I needed to clean it up. What was it that made the flash? I carefully chipped away the packed-on clay and dirt. I got a damp washcloth at the sink and continued to rub the artifact. It was beautiful under the crystal-clear covering. There were many colors of stone at different points around the circle with an "N" made of a glistening white stone. Then I noticed the hair-thin needle moving around the circle. It must be a compass!

"Tori! Timmy! It's time for dinner!" Mom called from the kitchen.

Suddenly my stomach rumbled and I could hear the growl for food. It had been all day since I had eaten. After all, that yellow stuff on the airplane plate that the flight attendant called lunch couldn't even be considered food. I quickly shoved the compass back into my pocket and headed for the kitchen, still feeling a little guilty that I had taken it from the dig site.

The three of us sat around the wooden dining table next to the small, narrow kitchen. I noticed the plate of thick, grilled burgers with a fresh bakery bun on each, some baked veggie chips, and a bowl of pineapple with an orange fruit.

"What's that?" Timmy asked as he took a huge bite.

"That's papaya. Do you like it?" giggled my mom as it was obvious he did.

Timmy, the piglet, was grabbing food like it was going out of style. He filled his plate and piled whatever he could find on top of his hamburger. He began inhaling his food like it was his last meal. All I could do was feel my stomach churn again when I looked at the juicy hamburgers. This time a different feeling came over me. Then I looked at my mom so she would know exactly what I thought.

"Mom, you don't care about me! Don't you know I'm a vegetarian?" I cried.

"What? When did this start? I can't keep up with you, Tori," responded my mom with an exasperated tone.

"You can't keep up with me? You're the one who left!" I shouted as I ran out of the house, slamming the door behind me.

Trying to catch my breath, I knew I needed some fresh air. I sat down on the rocking chair that looked so inviting on the front porch. My heart pounded hard through my chest. I had to get a grip on myself or this was gonna be a long six months. I could feel the thumps begin to slow as I took a big deep breath and could smell the strong perfume of the fragrant lei that still hung around my neck. It was then that I finally looked around.

The sky was a more vibrant blue than I'd ever seen before. In Michigan, the sky was typically a combination of shades of gray. Even the bluest of Michigan days paled in comparison to this blue Hawaiian sky. Then I noticed all the different sizes and shapes of palm trees. They looked so clean and almost like fake plastic. The sweet-smelling flowers that lined the grounds were various shades of bright pink, purple, orange, yellow, and red.

Noticing all this color reminded me of my colored pencils tucked away in my bag. Drawing was the one time I felt like I could escape from all the junk going on since Mom and Dad split up. I decided I would get started on my drawings first thing in the morning, right after I tried out the compass.

I wonder if the compass actually works?

CHAPTER 3

EMBARRASSING MOMENT

I could feel the kiss of the morning sun streaming in through the window and landing on my face. A gentle breeze coming through the open window forced me to open my eyes. It was then that I remembered where I was. I looked over at the bed next to me. Rumpled blankets and Timmy's stuffed dog were piled on top of the vacant bed. He had probably already gone exploring. Timmy seemed to have that more easygoing personality like Mom, but with the dark curly hair and deep blue eyes like Dad. Of course, I got the uptight personality of Dad, and Mom's thick, straight blonde hair. I didn't get her olive skin that tans so easily but my grandma's pink skin that burns. The clanking of dishes and the aroma of pancakes penetrating the air interrupted my thoughts.

Quietly, I started toward the kitchen. I stopped in my tracks when I heard my mom talking.

"Yes, Steve, the kids are fine. They're having a ball already," Mom said. "Yes, I know you called last night. We got your message. I'll let 'em know you called. Okay, goodbye."

I walked into the kitchen as she was slapping the pancakes onto the plates.

"Are you hungry?" she asked as if nothing had just happened.

"Mom? Was that Daddy on the phone?" I asked as I sat at the table.

"Oh, yeah. You can call him later."

"Weren't you going to tell me he called last night? I wanted to talk to him," I said.

"I just thought it would be better to wait until you were settled," Mom responded.

I was totally confused by Mom's actions sometimes. Why wouldn't she have told me right away that he called? Is she jealous of my relationship with Dad?

I began to dig in to the blueberry pancakes on my plate. They smelled so good, and I still hadn't eaten anything since the airplane yesterday. "Well, I'm gonna call him after breakfast."

"Fine. But you really have to watch how long you talk. The phone bill is very expensive."

"Daddy will pay. He said I could call him as much as I wanted on my cell phone he gave me, and you can't stop me," I said.

"I thought we might go to a luau tonight," suggested Mom, ignoring my last comment.

"What's a luau?"

"It's a traditional Hawaiian dinner party with hula and tribal dancing from the Polynesian heritage. It's at the community park tonight."

"I want to do my drawing today," I said.

"You still will have time for that. I thought it would be nice for you and Timmy to see some culture from the islands before starting school on Monday. Besides, Mr. Flannigan gave us tickets."

"Well, it looks like you made our plans already."

With that, we had plans for the evening. But in the meantime, I thought I could fit a lot of exploring and drawing into my day. But first, I would call Daddy.

I went to my room and called Dad's number on my cell phone.

*Ring-ring...ring-ring...*no answer.

I decided to leave a voicemail. "Daddy, it's me. Sorry I missed your call. I miss you! I will try to call again later. Love you!"

I carefully packed my drawing pad, colored pencils, a bottle of water, and a chocolate peanut butter snack bar in my backpack. Then I remembered the compass! I grabbed it out of the pants pocket I left it in last night and tucked it into the side pocket of my backpack. I couldn't wait to spend some time by

22

myself, drawing and studying the compass.

Once my backpack was securely fastened, I said goodbye and headed out. I started down the street thinking about how great it was to be alone and how I couldn't wait to find the perfect spot to begin drawing. I noticed a small house like the one we were staying in. I wondered if anyone lived there. It looked vacant. There were even some boards nailed across one of the front windows.

Behind the house I could see an opening in the thick green growth that led deeper into the valley. It looked like the most interesting path. I walked for a while as the land got steeper and steeper. I looked for rocks that were secure enough to hold my weight.

I could hear it before I saw it. As the land flattened out, I saw the most beautiful waterfall trickling into a small pool of the cleanest water I had ever seen. It was flowing into a stream that was surrounded by the most colorful flowers and twisted vines. I climbed up on a big flat rock that was at the bottom of the waterfall where I could see the whole beautiful scene without getting wet. This would be the perfect place to get out my drawing pad and get started. I looked at my watch and realized I'd only been walking for about thirty minutes. It was a short hike from the abandoned house. I decided not to tell my pain-in-the-neck brother about it so it could be *my* own special getaway.

I took the compass out of the side pocket to see which way I had come from and to inspect it a little closer. I held it flat on my palm and watched the needle spin around and around. It finally settled in one spot, so I turned the compass with the needle directly over the N like I had learned at school. Taking notice of where the path was, I concluded that I had come from the west. It was cool to see the compass work for real. I carefully set it down next to me on the big rock so I could begin drawing.

The colors on the page began to take on a life of their own. Teachers always told me that drawing was my "gift." I especially liked nature drawing. I had never seen such vibrant colors in Michigan, and it was amazing to really use every single color in my sixty-four-color pencil set on such a realistic drawing.

I was so absorbed in my drawing and taking in the beauty that time got away from me. I couldn't believe I'd been at the stream for so long! Mom was gonna kill me! The luau was at seven, and it was already six twenty. Oh, no! Gotta go!

I threw my pencils in my bag without putting them in the box. This was unusual for me since it is my pet peeve to have things out of place. Then I strapped the backpack on and began jogging down the path the way I had come. I hoped I would remember how to get to this magical place. It was the first time I had been able to actually forget how my family life had changed because of the stupid divorce.

I climbed back down toward the abandoned house when I remembered, the compass! I had to go back! I turned around and backtracked to the flat rock where I had been drawing. With a sigh of relief, I could see the shimmer of the compass before I reached it. I grasped it, quickly tossed it into the safety of the side pocket in my bag, and ran for home.

By the time I got back to the house, Mom had on a flowered sundress and Timmy was dressed in a wild and crazy flowered shirt I had never seen him in. He looked like he was going to be the clown entertainment at a party. I ran into my room to change and noticed there was a strange-looking something on my bed. I picked it up to get a closer look and realized it was a yellow and orange flowered sundress like Mom's. Oh brother. Doesn't she know anything? I haven't worn a dress since I started fifth grade! I put it on knowing that I didn't have a choice and I was late. I glanced at my reflection in the old, cracked mirror on the dresser and actually didn't look that bad. But wait! What's that on my forehead?

I moved closer to the reflection and noticed the biggest zit I had ever seen. I touched it and realized it was just at the beginning stages and I couldn't do anything about it. I had to do something. I found a tube of zit cream in my bag and dabbed some on, hoping it would disappear. When it didn't shrink instantly, I decided it wasn't the end of the world and I didn't know anyone anyway.

"Tori, are you ready yet?" hollered Mom.

"I'll be right there," I said as I finished brushing my hair and tying it quickly in a bun. Then I plucked a yellow flower out of the vase on the table and stuck it above my ear.

"Okay, now that looks like I'm goin' to a luau," I said aloud, remembering the picture on the cover of *Hawaiian Culture* magazine on the airplane.

We arrived at the community park and the parking attendant took the car to park it. Hawaiian music blared all around us. There were many long tables set up on a large patio decorated with flowers everywhere. I saw torches with big flames all the way around the park. I have to admit it looked kind of cool. Maybe as it got dark, no one would notice my zit. Just then Timmy turned to me and laughed, "Tori the unicorn!"

"What?" I was clueless what he was talking about.

"You have a big honkin' horn in the middle of your forehead!"

"You sticky glob of snot!" I cried.

"That's enough, you two," interrupted Mom. "Let's start by going through the food line and then find a seat at a table."

That sounded fine to me because once again, I was very hungry.

The food table was endless. There was so much food I didn't even recognize. It was colorful and smelled delicious. I noticed a lot of the exotic fruits, like pineapple, mango, papaya, and kiwi, in bowls scattered between all the platters of other foods. There was white rice, black rice, brown rice, and even blue rice! I saw purple sweet potatoes, too. Some vegetables I didn't even recognize.

The Hawaiian server who stood near the table answered questions and pointed out different things. She told me I should try poi, which was a very common Hawaiian vegetable. I slopped some onto the side of my plate. It didn't look very appetizing, but I decided it was time to expand my diet.

There were lots of different kinds of chicken and fish dishes. I loaded my plate with everything that looked edible. I don't mind eating fish, but I will never eat a poor little mammal or a bird again! I was able to make it all the way through the line without feeling queasy, even though I saw juicy meat on platters. Thank goodness the Hawaiians decorate the platters up so you can hardly tell what it is.

Mom said, "Follow me," as she led us to the table. Of course we were a little late, so the only spot with three places together was right up near the stage.

By the time we made it to our seats, all I heard was the beat of the tribal drums. The ground rumbled below me to the rhythm of the music.

Just then I looked up at the stage and saw three Hawaiian men beginning a dance. They were each dressed in something like a skirt that just hung in front and back but nothing on the sides. I couldn't believe my eyes. I don't even think they were wearing underwear.

They also had bare chests with necklaces made of big beads. They had something decorating their legs below the knee that looked like grass skirts, and they were wearing crowns made of green leaves. It was sort of scary sitting so close to the stage because it was loud, and they were stomping and yelling out strange grunts with the music.

Then the women took the stage. What a difference! They were all wearing red grass skirts that hung below their bellybuttons and had pompons attached. It was funny to see the pompons move so fast as their hips moved back and forth. I could never do that! All six of the hula dancers were pretty, with long black hair, and flowers on their heads and around their necks. This time the music wasn't so scary, or maybe I was just used to it.

The final act was the flame thrower! It was one of the guys who had been on stage before. This time he had something like Bella's baton in his hands, but both ends were on fire. I couldn't help but scoot my chair back a little farther. He started spinning the flaming baton around and around. He would throw it between his legs and then high up into the air.

"Well, what did you think?" asked Mom as the show ended.

"Awesome," was all I could say. Mom seemed to be relieved.

I overheard the man sitting behind us telling his family about the imu and pointed toward a crowd of people gathering at the edge of the far side of the patio. I decided I should go investigate.

"I'm gonna go see what's goin' on over there," I announced as I rushed to join the group.

I managed to shimmy my way through the crowd so I could get a front-row view of whatever we were there to see. Two men were in a big hole in the ground that was surrounded by rocks about the size of my fist. They each had a shovel and started moving sand that was covering something. They explained that the next layer was banana and ti leaves to keep the steam in. I wondered what we were about to see. Once the leaves were pulled off, steam rose and there were some orange coals below. Then, I got a good look. In fact, too good of a look! It was a whole pig that had been cooked in an oven! It was then I realized an imu was the open pit oven.

I looked at the pig's face and thought of Wilbur in *Charlotte's Web*. My stomach churned. I suddenly felt hot. And, I was trapped! There were too many people to get away. All I could do was feel my insides coming up through my throat.

And there it was…I puked right on the woman's foot that was standing behind me.

Then I felt as if everything froze in time. I noticed the woman's toe polish that matched the pink puke on her foot. I noticed the fingers pointing at me. I noticed the laughter and a few "gross" comments coming from the crowd.

This was my mom's fault. I covered my face as I ran to the car to wait for Mom and Timmy to notice I was missing and come find me. I waited and waited. They finally came, but I didn't talk to them the whole way home.

To think that a whole pig would be cooked that way! Did Mom not have a brain in her head to think I would enjoy that? All I wanted to do was go to bed so I could dream about the way things used to be.

CHAPTER 4

WAS IT A DREAM?

I ran to my room and once again threw myself on the bed. I hoped Timmy wouldn't come in for a while. Mom must have kept him busy so I could be alone because he stayed out. My eyes were getting heavy. They weighed a ton, and I couldn't keep them open any longer. Just as I was starting to drift off, I heard a rustling. I opened my eyes to see if Timmy had come in. Nope. I was still alone. But what was the noise?

My eyes closed again, and *whooosh!* A heavy breeze blew over me. Then it was gone! Weird. Is this house haunted? "What could go wrong now?" I asked.

"When things go wrong, as they sometimes will,
When the road you're trudging seems all uphill,
When care is pressing you down a bit,
Rest if you must, but don't you quit."

The voice bellowed, sounding like it was coming from a cave. I opened my eyes. *Flash.* But this time the light stayed. I couldn't believe what I was seeing and reached up to rub my eyes. I must've been dreaming.

～〇

The compass began to glow as its magnetized pointer quivered and pointed to the N for North. A bright light flashed out of the N, surrounded by a swirl of purple smoke. As the smoke faded away, the light dissolved into the mighty figure of a man wearing a long white cloak that was covered with a gold-embossed map of the world. Teeny, tiny gold sparkling compasses were dotted all over his cloak map. Hanging around his neck was a large gold compass medallion that looked just like the one he appeared out of. He grew to a height of nearly six feet five inches. With his thick curly mane of gold and red hair, he looked like the sun on fire. His full beard with ringlets and tiny braids sparkled when the light hit it just so. His eyes were a bright, bright blue and carried a never-ending twinkle in them as he surveyed his surroundings. His large face was kind and wise, and his lips parted underneath a gold-red curly mustache into a huge pearly white smile. He jumped away from the compass and landed on the floor with a sigh of relief. He twirled and danced with joy.

～〇

When I opened my eyes, I could see Timmy snuggled in a ball on his bed. He was making quiet sounds that meant he was fast asleep. My eyes darted

to where I had set the compass on the bedside table—
it was exactly as I had left it. Wow! That dream felt so
real. I rolled over and drifted back to sleep.

CHAPTER 5

SCHOOL DAYS

The next day was the day I'd been dreading since we got to the island. I had to start school. I felt tired from the night before. Had I been dreaming about the compass? Had I really seen a strange, magical man appear out of it? I really needed to get some good sleep.

I put on my cutest capri jeans and a T-shirt that said "Michigan." Timmy was the first one up, of course, and already talking excessively. I really think he needs a chill pill to come down to Earth. Daddy always said, "If we could only bottle and sell his energy, we would be rich." I totally get what he meant.

Mom drove us to school, like she would every morning.

"Kids, you will love this school! It looks a little different than the one you went to in Michigan. Some of the hallways are actually outdoors. Your cafeteria even has seating outside. Wait till you see the playground!"

Kauaiauai (ka-wa-ee-wa-ee) Elementary was a small school at the end of a quiet street. It was a one-story building that looked like four smaller buildings connected by outdoor hallways. In the center there was a courtyard with cafeteria-style tables. We made our way to the front office.

"Excuse me," Mom said, "I called to register my kids. We're here for the remainder of the year."

"Oh, yes, you must be the Chapmans?" inquired the secretary. She was native Hawaiian and was just about as big around as she was tall. Her friendly smile spread across her face from ear to ear. Her eyes sparkled with smile lines in each corner. "And you must be Tori, the fifth grader. I'm Mrs. Lawai." She stuck out her hand to shake mine. I had never been treated like I was an adult before, and it felt kind of good in a weird sort of way. "Your brother will be on the other end of the building in Mrs. Akela's third grade. You may go with this young lady to the fifth grade wing," she explained as she pointed to a beautiful native girl who stood about my height in the doorway of the office. "This is Leolana. She's in your class."

"Aloha," Leolana grinned. "You can call me Lana." Her shiny black hair hung straight down to the middle of her back. Her skin was the color of caramel, which accented her dark brown eyes nicely.

"Hi, I'm Tori." I tried to smile, but I was suddenly concerned that my zit was showing through my cover-up. We began to walk down the empty hall. Everyone else was already in class. We walked side by side, keeping stride with each other. Suddenly, she stopped and looked me in the eye.

"I remember you! You were at the luau last night!" she yelled.

"Yeah...where were you?" I asked.

"I was on stage at the beginning doing a dance with my dance group. But after that is when I saw you!"

Oh no! She couldn't have seen what I did, I thought.

"Aren't you the girl who puked on that lady at the pig roast?" she asked with a chuckle in her throat.

Just then a boy walked by and said, "You're the new haole (how-lee)!" without slowing down.

On that note, I decided that it was all going downhill from there. I had been spotted during the most embarrassing moment at the luau, and now I was already being called a name!

Lana chuckled. "Don't worry about him. That's Kyle, and he teases all the newbies. Haole is what the non-natives are called, and there are plenty of other haoles around."

"I thought Hawaii was part of the United States, but it seems so different," I said.

"It is. But it's full of culture from our ancestors. Where did you say you're from?"

"Michigan. The Great Lakes State," I said proudly.

"Maybe you can come with me this week to see what we do around here for fun," suggested Lana. "March is a great month to be here. Lots of fun stuff at school, but even more fun stuff around town!" We slowed down as we reached the classroom door with 21C on it. Above that appeared the name MRS. KAMEA. I must have looked at Lana with a question in my eyes because she smiled and said, "She's nice."

I followed Lana into the classroom and she addressed the teacher. "Aloha kakahiaka (kah-kah-hee-ah-kah). This is Tori from Michigan."

"Mahalo (Ma-ha-lo), Leolana. Aloha, Tori. I'm Mrs. Kamea. Please find the empty seat over there near the window," she said as she pointed to the vacant desk. There was a stack of books piled on top and I assumed they were for me. I began organizing them inside the desk.

Lana sat down at the desk right next to mine. Kids were reading quietly and I could feel their eyes follow me as I got situated.

The morning seemed to zoom by. Mrs. Kamea was starting a new unit in reading: historical fiction. This sounded interesting. We began reading a book that was based in Hawaii during the bombing of Pearl Harbor. After she read a couple of chapters to us, we had to write in a reading journal about what we visualized. I began a pencil sketch of a bird's-eye view of my vision of Pearl Harbor.

Lana peeked over my shoulder and commented, "Wow! Have you been there? That almost looks like a black and white photograph!"

Just then there was a stampede of kids coming toward my desk wanting to see the drawing. I felt the room spin as the blood rushed to my head. I was embarrassed, and I wanted to leave. I have always kept my drawings to myself, well, except for sharing with art teachers. Then I heard, "Not bad for a haole!"

Oh no! That rude kid, Kyle, was in this class. I couldn't believe I hadn't noticed him yet. A strange bell went off. The kids all began to clear their desks and line up to go to lunch.

On the way to the lunch room, Lana introduced me to two of her other friends, Kiki and Lisa. Kiki was another native Hawaiian, but Lisa was blonde and looked a little more like me.

"Tell us about yourself," said Lisa as if she were interviewing me.

"I'm from Michigan, but I'm here for six months while my mom is on a boring archaeological dig," I answered.

"Are there any cute boys in Michigan?" she giggled.

Cute boys? Who cares about boys?

"Most boys are a pain," I said.

"Lisa is boy crazy," laughed Lana.

Kyle walked by to go to the trash can. I noticed he could have gone a shorter way, but instead he walked right by our table. Lisa looked at him, tilted her head sideways, and flung her long, silky blonde blond hair over her shoulder. Oh, I get it! Lisa likes Kyle.

"The boys are all Lisa crazy, too!" Kiki added.

By the end of lunch, I knew about all the cool boys, geek boys, jock boys, and brainy boys.

The afternoon dragged because I had had enough newness for the day. I wanted to go home, get the compass, and go exploring some more. I left the compass in my underwear drawer because I didn't want to take a chance of losing it at school.

At the end of the day, Lana caught up with me in the hall, "Hey, Tori, how 'bout tomorrow you plan to come to my house after school?" she asked.

"That would be fun. I'll let you know."

I walked out the front of the school and stood on the steps waiting for Timmy. While I waited, I decided I may as well check my phone to see if Dad had called me back. Sure enough! The red light blinked indicating that I had a text. It was from Dad!

Hey Angel, I've been crazy with meetings. I'll call the first chance I get. Time change is tough. Love you. Love to Timmy, too!

My knees buckled as someone pressed behind

them. I turned around to find Timmy there with a great big smile. He always did stuff like that to make me mad.

"What are you doing? You could have made me fall!" I yelled.

"What are you so mad about?" Timmy asked. "Didn't you like your new class?"

"It was fine. What about you? Did they figure out you're a pain in the neck yet?"

"Ha, ha! Very funny. As a matter of fact, all the kids wanted to play with me at recess. I was the best soccer player!"

We could see the little yellow compact drive up in front of the school. Mom was looking around trying to spot us. When she did, she raised her eyebrows and smiled as if to ask, how was your day? We piled into the car, and, of course, Timmy started in about his day and his amazing soccer skills. Then she looked over to me. "Tori, what about you?"

"It was okay. I met a friend named Lana."

"Really? That's great! Is that the girl who walked you to class?"

"Yes. She wants me to go over to her house tomorrow."

"That would be nice one of these days, soon."

"Why not tomorrow?" I asked.

"As I told you before, I have some deadlines this

week. And tomorrow I need you to watch Timmy after school."

"That's not fair!" I shouted. "I finally am ready to try to get along out here and you always have to wreck everything!"

As soon as we got home, I grabbed my backpack, drawing pad, and pencils, and the compass from my underwear drawer. I headed out. It was not fair that she was always getting in the way of my plans.

CHAPTER 6

COMPASS MYSTERY

I slowed down when I got closer to the abandoned house. Today I thought would be a good day to explore there. I softly stepped up on the porch steps, careful to skip the sections with loose boards. *Creeeak*, I heard the porch as I tiptoed across it. The windows were boarded up, but the door looked like it was inviting me in. It was loosely closed and I only needed to push it since the doorknob was missing.

The sun streamed through the boarded windows inside the living area. There wasn't any furniture, except for an old stand-up mirror in the corner and a couple of worn-out chairs in the main room. I decided that this would be a great place to sit and inspect the compass a little more. I felt it getting warm in my pocket again. I wondered what it was that made it turn warm.

I took it out and watched the needle dance around in circles until it quivered to a stop. This time it stopped directly on the N without my turning the compass. I sat down on the ratty stuffed chair and looked closer. A bright light began to flash from the N just like in my dream. At least I thought it was a dream! I set the compass down on the floor next to me, afraid of what might happen next. I pulled out my drawing pad to begin to draw my observations.

I took a big deep breath and again noticed the sunlight gleaming through the window. Maybe that was where the flash of light came from. My eyelids began to get heavy, and I drifted off to sleep.

I woke with a start when I felt a chill brush up against my face. When I opened my eyes there was a swirl of purple smoke. It looked like a slow-moving purple tornado. As the smoke faded away, the figure I'd seen in my dream stood in front of me.

My heart skipped a beat as the stranger stood so tall above me. "Stay away from me!" I screamed as I scrunched my body into a tight ball, covered my eyes for protection, and prepared myself for what might come next.

"What are you doing? Get out of here!" I cried and pinched my arm to wake myself up from this horrible dream.

The man with the white cloak smiled at me and cooed in the most comforting voice.

"Child, don't be frightened. You seem so lost. I am here to help you find your way."

"H-h-help me find my w-w-way? Where am I going?" I stammered. "I don't want to go anywhere with you!"

"No, dear child. Metaphorically speaking, you are lost. Not really physically lost. You have so much anger built up that needs to be released before you can find your way to happiness."

"Who are you? Where did you come from?" I asked. What makes him think he knows so much about me?

"Please excuse my rudeness. I am Father North, and I am Keeper of the Right Path. When one of the children of the world loses their way from the Right Path, I assist in various ways," Father North explained.

I should have been frightened, but I wasn't for some strange reason. His voice was so friendly, and his eyes had a familiar never-ending twinkle.

Father North moved closer to me. He reminded me of my grandfather. I didn't say anything, but my face must have given away my thoughts because he continued.

"Tori, I would like for you to try something. You need to open your eyes and look around you. You are missing some important things due to the blindness of your anger."

He grasped the compass around his neck and rubbed the glass front in a swirly pattern of some sort.

A purple swirl surrounded it as it grew into a looking glass. There was an image. He held it out for me to get a better look. Inside the looking glass compass a misty scene appeared. Then it became clear, like I was looking into the next room.

My mom was smiling as she checked on Timmy. Then she went into her bedroom and closed the door. Suddenly I could see her sitting on her bed. She stared at the closed door and then her face got very sad. She covered her face with her hands, and I could see her shoulders move up and down. She was crying!

Then the scene faded.

"What was that about?" I asked.

"Tori, you have been thinking only about how these changes between your mom and dad have affected you. You haven't even realized how it has affected others," Father North explained.

"Is this all my fault?" Tears burned my eyes.

"No, Tori. This is where you need to listen closely. Your parents' divorce is an adult issue. It has nothing to do with you or Timmy. Both of your parents love you and want you to be happy."

"But…when they fought it always started with something I did!" I cried.

"No, it didn't. That is what you thought you saw. Please take another look." Father North rubbed the compass again with his fancy pattern.

In the glass were Timmy and me a couple years ago. I remembered this night like it was yesterday. We had just come home from the school carnival. We had blue cotton candy on our teeth and fingertips. We were laughing and having a great time. We went to get our PJs on. Then I saw what I hadn't seen before. Dad approached Mom quietly and said, "This is not working. We are going through the motions, but we don't love each other anymore. It's time to move on." Mom looked at him with tears in her eyes.

"You're right. We just don't see eye to eye on things anymore. Obviously, all the counseling we did just isn't making a difference."

When Timmy and I came back into the living room, Mom and Daddy were both screaming. They noticed blue fingerprints on the walls and the white couch. They were yelling about how they couldn't keep anything nice. We wrecked everything!

The image faded once again. I looked at Father North with a question in my eyes.

"Yes, Tori, they were working on their marriage for quite some time. They wanted to make it work for you and Timmy, but they realized that it was better for all of you to move on. Don't you want happiness for both your mom and dad?"

"Of course I do. But—"

"No buts. You should learn that sometimes the

path of life you're on has little detours along the way. Detours aren't a bad thing. They just help you get around something that needs fixing. Your parents tried patching the path for a while but have now learned that they need to pave a new path. You need to help others around you. Understand, you will all get through this," Father North promised.

I nodded my head in understanding. Again, my eyes felt heavy, so I laid my head down on the ratty chair and drifted off to sleep.

When I woke a while later, the compass was still sitting on the floor where I had set it. I looked at my drawing pad and noticed that I had just begun drawing the compass with a purple smoke swirl surrounding it.

So Father North was not a dream after all! I smiled to myself, knowing what I must do now.

CHAPTER 7

OPEN EYES

When I walked through the door of my home after my amazing visit to the abandoned house, I decided to sit in the living room instead of going straight to my room. The house was as clean and tidy as it could be. All the furniture looked worn, but it was all very tropical. There were native-looking art sculptures and paintings hanging on the walls, and there was one shelf that had to have at least twenty pictures of Timmy and me at different stages of our lives. Some of the pictures had a hole cut in them, which made me sad to think that Dad had been not only cut out of the pictures but also out of our lives. I couldn't believe I had been here for almost a week and I hadn't even noticed all this! I wondered if this was what Father North meant by "Open your eyes. Look around you."

I heard Timmy before he and Mom reached the front door. When they noticed me sitting in the living room, Timmy asked, "What are you doing here?"

"What do you mean...Timmy?" I asked while trying to hold back from using my usual nicknames.

"Why aren't you pouting or doing something in your room?" he said.

I ignored him and turned to my mom. "Mom, I was just looking at all these pictures. We had a lot of fun, didn't we?"

"Yes, we did," she said as she walked toward the shelf and picked up a snowy picture. "Remember this when we would go skiing in northern Michigan?"

"Yes, all the trips with the framily," I added, using the family nickname for our group of lifelong friends that we would often travel with.

"Remember staying in the cabin at the bottom of Mount Superior, when the bear that knocked on the window tripped over the trash cans?" I added laughing.

Mom chuckled. "Yes, but it wasn't funny until the next day when we knew we were safe."

"Then remember when we went canoeing with the family? And Tori and Bella saw the big turtle that made them freak out!" said Timmy. "They flipped that canoe right over when they were screaming like babies!"

"What about when Dad was telling us what to do if we saw a bear when we were hiking at Yosemite National Park? He made us practice being calm and quiet. Then, when Mom heard a twig break, she thought it was a bear and screamed out of her wits and ran so fast she left us behind!" I reminded them. It felt so good to laugh with Mom and Timmy, even if it lasted only a couple of minutes. WOW! We've shared a lot of good times. I really do love my family.

Mom and Timmy had brought home pizza for dinner, which I seemed to enjoy more than usual. I guess this was what they meant when they say, "laughter is the best medicine."

As we were finishing up dinner, the house phone rang.

"Hello?" Mom said into the phone.

"Hi, Steve, yes...Here's Tori." She handed me the phone and said, "I guess Dad couldn't reach you on your cell phone."

"Hi, Daddy!"

"Hi, Angel. How are things going?" he asked.

"They're okay. I miss home already."

"Well, I'm sure the weather is much nicer there. It's been storming here for the past three days, and all the detours of the spring construction make it frustrating on the roads. But the new roads will be so much nicer. Tell me about YOU!"

I went on telling him about the luau and the first day of school and then gave the phone to Timmy. I thought about what he said about the detours. That's what Father North said! The new roads will be much nicer!

I wonder if I'm supposed to help "pave the road"?

CHAPTER 8

SURF'S UP

The next day the idea of school seemed easier since the whole scene was more familiar. I decided that I better not leave my compass behind, so I tossed it into my shorts pocket on the way out. I wanted to be sure to be near it in case Father North made another appearance.

When Mom dropped us off at school, she reminded me, "Tori, don't forget, I need you to watch Timmy today. I will be in a meeting. Do you think you can remember the way home?"

"Yes, Mom. I remember. It's only a couple of turns. We won't get lost," I assured her as I patted my pocket containing the compass.

"Bye sweethearts! Have a nice day!" she cheered.

"Bye Mom, you too!" said Timmy as he slammed the door and ran to the school.

I slammed the door as I quietly said, "Love you," knowing quite well that she didn't hear me. It was a step in the right direction, though. It was always hard telling my mom I loved her. I was so mad at her because she was always leaving for her job. In fact, her being gone so much didn't help our family stay together.

As I ran up to the front steps of the school, I noticed Lana carrying a large box. I joined her and said, "Hey! Can I help you?"

"Sure, thanks!"

"What's all this?" I asked as I peeked in.

"It's artifacts for the Cultural Day that's coming up. My mom is very involved in PTA and wanted me to give it to Mrs. K."

"You're lucky that your mom likes to get involved," I said. Mom was always too busy working to help at school.

After dropping off the box with Mrs. K, we headed to our classroom.

The morning seemed to fly by. In fact, math was never my strongest subject, but Mrs. K made it fun. You would never even know we were learning math! She had us draw pictures using a protractor. We had to use certain sizes of angles. By the time my drawing was finished, people were already peeking over my shoulder. My drawing had turned into a beautiful lacy snowflake. It reminded me of Michigan.

In social studies, we were learning about World War II and the bombing of Pearl Harbor. It was perfect timing since we were doing the same in our historical fiction unit. I got to see a real photograph of Pearl

Harbor, and it did look just like my drawing from yesterday. How freaky.

Before long the bell rang to get ready for lunch. All the kids cleared their desks and quickly lined up. I rushed to get in line near Lana. Suddenly, I felt a shove in my back as it pushed me into the wall. I turned around and it was Kyle! This was going to get old. I bent my elbow and jammed it into his side. He yelled out, "Mrs. K, Tori just pushed me!" I couldn't believe it! I never get in trouble. But here came Mrs. K.

"Tori, please take the end of the line. We don't act like that at Kauiaui Elementary." I hung my head as I walked to my new place. By the time we got to the lunch room, I was so embarrassed I just wanted to sit alone.

Lana and Kiki ran up to me and giggled. "What are you doing, Tori? Don't worry about Kyle. He is crushing on you bad!"

"What? The kid that has called me names, shoved me, and tattled on me has a crush on me?" I asked. I remember my mom always telling me that boys acted weird when they liked you, but I didn't know that meant annoying.

Lisa walked by without saying a word to me. In fact, if I didn't know better, I might have thought she was ignoring me! She sat at the other end of the table with some other girls I hadn't met yet.

"Oh, my gosh! Lisa is jealous of you, Tori!" exclaimed Lana.

"She just wants to be the only one that the boys look at," added Kiki.

I glanced over my shoulder to see the group of girls she was sitting with, and all at once they began to laugh at something she said while they looked my way. Oh no! She must be talking about me! I couldn't believe the sinking feeling in my stomach.

Lana and Kiki continued to talk all through lunch about boys and things that were going on. All I could do was smile as I thought about Kyle with the dark curly hair and how he liked me!

The afternoon continued to go rather fast. Before long the final bell rang and kids began to rush down the hall to head out of the building. I headed to the front door to meet Timmy and begin walking home. Lana caught up with me.

"Hey, Tori, aren't you coming over?" she asked.

"Oh, sorry. I have to babysit today. Maybe another time."

"Bring Timmy! Please, please! I wanted to show you the best thing about Hawaii today," Lana pleaded. "The waves will be perfect to see some great surfing."

"Well, I guess I could bring Timmy. As long as we're home by six," I said, knowing that Mom would never approve.

Beep beep we heard from a green SUV parked in front of the school with a surfboard attached to the top. I could see a boy behind the driver's seat who looked barely sixteen. Lana started to run toward the car.

"Come on! That's my brother, James," she yelled behind her. Timmy and I followed her. As she climbed in, she said, "Hi, James, this is my new friend Tori and her brother Timmy."

"Hi. Hop in and we will show you where the action is," he said, smiling politely.

"Nice to meet you." I got comfortable in the back seat. Timmy grasped my arm without saying a word. I could tell he was a little scared. I guess I was a little unsure of things, too. After all, I'd only met Lana yesterday.

As we drove into the parking lot at the beach, I saw car after car filing in. I guess this was the place to be. We got out and walked along the powdery sand until we came to a spot where people were gathering. We decided to sit and watch. James started to wax his surfboard with the other surfers.

"See the red flag?" asked Lana. "That tells us that the surf is up and it'll be big waves!"

There were surfers everywhere! We watched as they ran to the water, paddled their surfboards into the waves, and balanced as they stood with confidence.

"Awesome," Timmy sighed.

"Do you want to get your feet wet?" I asked, knowing that Timmy was uncomfortable around the water. When he was little he was knocked down by a big wave in Lake Michigan and he thought he was going to drown. He hadn't been swimming since.

"I don't know…" he said as if deep in thought.

"We can just go walk on the wet sand?" I suggested.

"Okay…I guess I can do that."

Timmy and I walked slowly toward the water. Waves crashed against a rock formation to our right, and we could see the spray of water high in the air. On our left were the surfers coming and going on the wet sand. We found a spot where no one was. Timmy stood on the wet sand and smiled.

"Look, Tori! I'm sinking in quicksand!" His feet disappeared until the wet sand was halfway up his calf. Then we held hands as we played tag with the waves. As the water would go out, we would run as far as we could before the water returned to chase us back up on the beach.

We ran back and forth pulling each other at least ten times before we fell to the sand in laughter. Our school clothes were soaked, but we didn't care. Timmy and I were actually having fun together! Again, the laughter made me feel lighter somehow.

We walked back to the sitting area. Lana was wearing her swimsuit and had a surfboard under her arm. Wow! I couldn't believe Lana was going to surf, too.

"Here goes! Wish me luck!" Lana yelled as she ran toward the waves. She paddled her board out to catch up with James. Together they moved toward the big wave, timing it perfectly. They held onto each other's arms as they stood on their boards. Then, an amazing thing happened! James picked up Lana and she was on his shoulders.

"Oh my gosh! They're pros!" I exclaimed.

"That's epic! I want to do that someday," said Timmy with awe.

"Well, you're on your way, Timmy. Just think how you got your feet wet today!"

"Thank you, Tori. I wouldn't have done it without you."

I ruffled his curly brown hair and thought to myself that he wasn't a bad kid. I shouldn't be so hard on him.

It seemed we were there for such a short time, but it was already after five thirty. I knew we had to get home before Mom. I went to find Lana as she and James were walking up the beach.

"Lana, we need to get going," I said.

"Bummer! Do you need a ride?" she asked.

"Yes, we have to be home by six."

Lana grabbed her brother and they quickly loaded up the SUV to head home. It was already ten to six, so it was going to be close. After the surfboards were attached to the roof, James quickly jumped behind the driver's seat.

"Okay, where to?" he asked.

"I only know my way back from the school," I answered.

With that, he drove out of the parking lot and headed toward the school. It was looking more familiar now. I directed James down the curvy road to our house. I saw the house in the distance as I noticed my watch said 6:01. Phew! We made it! Or did we? What is that yellow car doing in the driveway? Did Mom come home early? What are we going to do? My heart was beating faster as I prepared to meet the circumstances of my mom.

"Thanks, James and Lana! It was fun. It was nice knowing ya! Now my mom's gonna kill me," I said as I closed the door and waved.

"That was wicked! Thank you, thank you!" yelled Timmy.

As the green SUV pulled out, I felt Mom's eyes glaring at me through the window. I walked up the steps and was greeted at the door with, "Where have you been? Who were you with? What were you thinking?"

"Mom, It's just that—" I began.

"It's just that nothing! You were supposed to be babysitting your brother after school!" continued Mom.

"Well, Lana told me I could bring Timmy. She wanted to show us the surfing that all the kids do around here," I explained.

"There are so many reasons why this was wrong," she continued. "You were *told* to take Timmy straight home. You only met Lana yesterday. Her brother hardly looked old enough to drive! The ocean is a dangerous place! Your brother almost drowned a few years ago!" She covered her face with her hands and cried, "I was so worried!"

I reached out and put my hand on her shoulder. "You don't trust me, Mom. I was babysitting him. And, as you can see, he's fine! Why don't you trust me?"

Timmy interrupted, "Mom, you should have seen it! The surfers were awesome! And you'll never guess what happened!" He paused and said, "I went in the water!"

She uncovered her face and looked at Timmy in astonishment.

"What?" she asked for clarification.

"I went in the water with Tori. We played tag with the waves. But can you believe it? I was brave enough with Tori there to do it! I want to learn to surf!"

My mom looked at me in amazement. We didn't think Timmy would ever go near the water while we were in Hawaii. She reached out with both arms and pulled Timmy and me to her.

"I'm sorry I disappointed you," I said.

"You don't disappoint me. I was just so worried about you both," she whispered as she hugged us close. "I would die if anything ever happened to you."

I could feel the warmth in my pocket. I had almost forgotten about the compass. Does Father North think I'm on the right track?

CHAPTER 9

FLIRTING?

The next week at school was crazy busy. I was still getting adjusted to my new teachers, the outdoor lunchroom, and of course Kyle picking on me. But now every time he called me "haole" or pushed me, I just played along. It's funny now that my eyes were opening to all that was going on around me, I noticed how Kyle would always choose to sit near me on the floor with his knee touching mine or stand near me in line.

Every morning Mrs. Kamea would start the day the same way.

"Aloha kakahiaka!"

And the class would respond, "Aloha, Mrs. Kamea!"

On this particular day, Mrs. Kamea looked at me and said, "Tori, you came at an exciting time of year. Here at Kauiaui Elementary as we celebrate history month, we are preparing for our annual Cultural Day in April and the Historical Art Fair in May."

I smiled to myself when I heard the words "art

63

fair." I had always wished my old school would have one, but we usually focused on the science fair.

"Speaking of art, it's time to line up to go to art class," announced Mrs. Kamea.

"Yes!" the class said in unison. It was obvious everyone loved going to art. I grabbed my drawing pad just in case we had extra time to draw.

Kyle of course rushed to line up behind me. It was the usual order: Lana in front of me and Kyle behind. I felt the familiar irritating footsteps too close to mine causing the back of my sandal to fly off.

"Stop it, Kyle!" I yelled. He snickered as he tried to repeat with the other foot. "It's not funny," I said with a little chuckle.

"Why ya laughin' then?" he asked. We reached the art room and were expected to stand at attention until the art teacher, Mrs. Waters, let us in.

"Don't dare act up for Mrs. Waters because she will pull you out of art for sure," Lana whispered. We all filed in and went to our assigned seats. I didn't get to sit near Lana or Kyle because we had been separated the first week I was here.

"Okay, class, as you know, we have the art fair coming up in a couple of weeks. Your assignment is to use any of the artistic media we learned about this year," Mrs. Waters explained. "To stick with the theme of history, you need to think about what has changed your history. You may draw it, paint it, sculpt it, photograph it, or use your creative imagination."

"Cool," I said as I looked at the boy sitting next to me. His name was Sam and he wasn't a very good student. I wondered if he would be better at art than the other subjects. I watched his expression, which didn't change underneath his long hair hanging in his eyes. He didn't appear to care about the assignment. He just wanted to get it over with.

I chose the charcoal pencils to use for my drawing. I didn't need to think about what had changed my history—it was the divorce and how we would never be that happy family again.

"What kind of object can change your history?" I asked myself aloud without thinking about Sam sitting across from me.

"My Xbox changed my history!" he answered. I couldn't help but frown at him.

"How would that change history?" I asked.

"I play games instead of watch TV," he said like a know-it-all.

Ignoring Sam, I randomly opened up my sketch pad to see if I could get any ideas. The first place it opened to was the compass with the purple tornado coming out of it. I flipped through the pages and saw the waterfall I liked to visit. Next was the airplane I had flown on. Then there was a sketch I had done a long time ago of Mom and Dad. Finally, there was the big maple tree and tree house in our backyard in Michigan. All of these things were important to me in some way, but what had changed my history? I closed the book. I opened it one more time and again it opened right on the compass page. That's it! It must be the compass! Now how could a compass change history or change my history?

I began drawing a new sketch of the compass on a clean piece of paper from Mrs. Waters's shelf. The clear memory stuck in my brain, so I didn't even have to take the compass out of my pocket. I drew the different precious stones that were inlaid throughout. I drew the hair-thin needle pointing to the N. I drew the reflection off the glass as I had seen it coming from the boarded-up windows, carefully adding every detail in various shades of charcoal. Finally, I decided it needed a splash of color. I grabbed a piece of purple chalk. That would be the purple tornado.

Suddenly, I saw a blur in the side of my eye. I turned my head and saw Kyle opening my drawing pad!

"NO!" I yelled.

"Ooooo, look at this!" he said as he pointed to the waterfall and ran between the desks with my drawing pad. I stood up and chased him to the end of the classroom.

"Stop it!" I said as I could feel the sting in my eyes from the tears I tried to hold back.

"A haole can draw! Is this your mom and dad?" he asked as he turned the pages.

This was too much! I couldn't hold it back any longer. I punched him on the arm, grabbed the drawing pad, and went into the hall to cry. How could this guy do this if he liked me?

It wasn't long until Mrs. Waters came out into the hall to investigate what had happened. My shoulders shook as I tried to catch my breath. It was obvious I had been crying like a baby.

"Oh, Tori, you'll be okay," she said in a calm voice. "What did Kyle do to upset you so?"

With one more big breath I answered, "He took my drawing pad and was looking all through it."

"And that upset you? Did he make fun of your drawing?"

"No, he just looked at all my private stuff. This is like a diary to me. I don't share it with anyone," I explained. "Not even my mom."

"You're very talented, and you should be proud of what you can do. I understand that it felt like he was invading your space. I will talk with Kyle about how it hurt your feelings. I'm sure he didn't want to hurt you." Mrs. Waters made me feel better.

As I walked back into the classroom and cleaned

up my pencils, I hoped I could get the project done by the due date. We stacked our artwork on racks so they wouldn't get smudged. Kyle just looked at me from a distance as if he was afraid to get too close. He didn't line up or sit near me for the rest of the day.

CHAPTER 10

CULTURAL DAY

The whole school was completely prepared for Cultural Day. Many parents were bringing artifacts and food from their heritage to share. We had countries represented like Japan, India, Germany, New Zealand, and Australia. But most of the stuff came from the Polynesian Islands. I learned that Hawaii's native people were from many different Polynesian Islands.

We were so excited to leave our class for the whole afternoon to visit the exhibits. There was a rotating schedule that all the classes went through. Many of the stations were set up in the outdoor cafeteria. Other stations were in the media center and the gym. The food smelled delicious. When we got to the Polynesian music station, I couldn't help but notice Lana's big smile. She grabbed my arm and took me to the table holding all the interesting-looking instruments.

"Mom, this is Tori, my new friend I told you about," introduced Lana.

"Nice to meet you, Tori. How do you like your new school?" asked her mom.

"Oh, it's cool. Nice to meet you, Mrs. Lai," I said politely.

I looked at the different wooden instruments on the table. There were also a few different wooden drums that were all different sizes. I recognized a small stringed instrument like my dad had.

Mrs. Lai explained, "These are ukuleles with eight strings. Here is one from Tahiti made from native wood, and this one is a koa ukulele made from a local wood from Hawaii." She picked up the koa ukulele and began to play a tune. It sounded like the hula music from the luau. The kids all sat down and listened to her play. Then another mom began playing on the drums. I noticed Lana's mom look at her and raise her eyebrows as if asking Lana something. Just then, Lana stood up and put on the grass skirt that was lying on the table. She began to hula in front of the class! How brave. But I guess she was used to it. She explained how the hand signals in the dance tell a story. My knee felt the warmth of Kyle's leg as it brushed against mine. The incident in art was long forgotten and we were back to sitting near each other whenever we could.

After that, we went out to the courtyard where there were several other stations. There was a big crowd around a station that I couldn't see. Then I noticed a big sign that read "Artifacts of Kauai." I wondered what was so exciting. I slowly squeezed between the crowd and made my way so I could see.

What? It couldn't be!

There was my mom holding up artifacts and talking about them! She didn't even tell me she was going to be there. I felt tears well up in my eyes. Why am I crying?

I knew they were tears of joy. She had never been able to help at my old school. I knew now that my mom was trying the best she could. I listened as she talked about the pottery and part of a canoe that had been found in the archaeological dig.

As I got closer to the table, a smile spread across my face. Her look told me she had accomplished her mission. She had attempted to make a difference in my day. And she had.

Later, Kiki ran up to me. "Tori, your mom is so cool! She really knows a lot about the history of Hawaii."

"Really? I never put my mom in the 'cool' category," I replied. "But I guess she's not bad."

"Not bad? She actually could tell me some of the background of my great ancestors! She knew all about the Asian and French bringing canoes to the islands. She also showed me some Lapita pottery! That's pottery that has been around since 2,500 B.C.!"

"Wow! People have been on this island since then?" I asked.

"Yeah. Your mom said that they found their way to the islands by using the stars as maps," continued Kiki. "But then, she was on a dig and someone found a compass!"

My stomach dropped to the floor. What did she say? They found a compass? Did they know it was missing?

"Rrrreally? A compass?" I asked for clarification.

"Yes, it was on the table with the pottery."

I quickly felt my pocket; the compass was gone! Oh no! I turned and quickly did a walk-run through the hall back to the courtyard where the artifacts station had been. Everything was already cleaned up! I couldn't even think straight.

The dismissal bell rang and the hall filled with screaming kids. I felt the urge to get out of there and go to the old abandoned house.

I raced down the hall to find Timmy. I had to get out of there *now*! We jogged all the way home. Surprisingly, Timmy didn't even ask why.

When Timmy and I rushed into our house, Mom was there with all of the artifacts. I immediately walked up to the box of artifacts on the kitchen table and started scanning the items for the compass.

"Hi, Tori. Why the sudden interest in the artifacts?" asked Mom.

"Kiki was talking about all the cool stuff you

knew about it. You never told me all that stuff."

"You never seemed interested before," she replied. "I would be happy to show you around the dig site if you want."

"That would be great sometime. Kiki mentioned a compass. Is it here?" I asked as I began my own "dig" in the box. My mom carefully pulled the box toward her and began gently taking items out. Then she pulled out a plastic box. She clicked the box open and there it was. A dirty old compass that had clay and dirt still stuck on it.

"Is this what you wanted to see?" she asked as she held it out. There was a feeling of relief, as well as confusion, when I saw that it was a compass that looked just like the one I had taken. But I had already cleaned it up, and this looked like it was fresh from the dig.

"Cool. What do you know about the compass?" I asked.

"This compass looks like it dates back about two thousand years. Unfortunately, the needle doesn't spin. But it tells us that there were more advanced sailors in that time than we originally thought. The compass originated in China, we thought, around the year 1050. But this one here appears to be even older."

"Interesting. Thanks for sharing, Mom. I'm going to go do some drawing, okay?"

I ran to my room to see if my compass was in my underwear drawer. No luck. My shorts from yesterday and the day before sat on the floor in a pile. Quickly grabbing both pairs, I checked each pocket carefully. Still nothing. I crawled under my bed and checked with all the cobwebs. What the heck? I couldn't wait to get to the abandoned house to see if my compass was there.

CHAPTER 11

OPEN TOUCH

I grabbed my bag with drawing pad and pencils and headed out. When I got to the abandoned house, I took the steps two at a time. The door was open just a crack, as it had been before. The house seemed empty, and the light didn't shine through the window boards as it had before. I surveyed my surroundings to see if I had left the compass on the floor or in the chair where I had been sitting. Nothing!

I sat down on the ratty stuffed chair and laid my head on the chair arm. I was exhausted and began to get sleepy. Then it happened. A purple tornado seeped from my book bag. I couldn't believe it. I had the compass with me all along. Father North appeared from the purple tornado. He seemed to have a grin in his eyes with the twinkle that wouldn't go away.

"My dear Tori, what a good student you are. You learn so quickly," he said in his soothing voice. "Can you tell me something you have already learned?"

"Thank you, Father North," I said. "Laughing sort of felt good instead of yelling."

"Yes, child. You will see that when you surround yourself with laughter and search for the good in things, good things will come." I sat up straight so I could hear my next assignment.

Father North continued, "You have started to let your brother into your life a little bit by including him with your friends and helping him get over his fear of water. He is grateful to you. You have shared a little laughter with your mom and showed some interest in her job. Those are both very big steps in the right direction. Now you need to let your mother into your world. Think about what is important to you and share it with her. This will lead you to more open communication with her."

I had to ask. "Father North, my mom had another compass that looked just like yours. Do they know this compass is missing? I feel like it was wrong to take it."

"Dearest Tori, you were meant to take the compass on that first day you were here. Our paths were meant to cross. Have no worries. I made a duplicate to replace it so it wouldn't be missed."

"Where did the compass come from?"

"The compass and I have been buried here for two thousand years, waiting to be found. You have unlocked the secret, and I am here to help guide you and get you on the Right Path."

"Thank you, Father North." With that, I drifted

off to sleep. A little while later I woke up and my stomach was growling. I grabbed my bag, making sure the compass was still inside, and skipped home.

CHAPTER 12

COINCIDENCE

Saturdays were always days I looked forward to. Usually Mom would go into work for the morning and Timmy and I would sleep in. The rest of the day would be for exploring and drawing. Today was different. Mom didn't have to work, so she got us up early for a surprise hiking trip. My mom always liked the outdoors and was good at adventure.

"Be sure to wear your hiking shoes and get your backpacks so you can pack plenty of water," Mom hollered to us both.

"Where are we going?" I asked.

"Oh, I can't tell you or it wouldn't be a surprise!" she giggled.

Timmy was already dressed with his floppy hiking hat pulled down over his ears. He had his backpack, a walking stick he found behind the house, and a great big smile on his face. I was happy to see him smile.

We loaded all our hiking gear into the car. When the dig site was in view, I guessed we were going on an archaeological dig. Boy, was I wrong. She parked at the dig site, unloaded the car, and began walking toward the mountain. We passed all of the little squares labeled with letters and numbers. After reaching the mountain's base, we began the steep climb. There was a narrow path that had tree roots every once in a while that we used as steps. It seemed like we were walking for a long time when suddenly the trees opened up and we could see a perfect view of the ocean. It was so blue!

"Wow!" was all I could say.

"Isn't it beautiful? So untouched by civilization," Mom said.

"Why do people have to ruin everything?" Timmy asked as I thought the same.

"People always seem to want to speed things up with their inventions. Of course, everything used to make inventions comes from the earth. Hawaii is rich in natural resources. Hawaiians have done a fabulous job of conserving the land." Mom always sounded like a teacher.

We climbed a little higher until the mountain began to level off. Mom led us down the other side. We only reached about halfway down that side of the mountain when Mom turned and smiled. A cave was hidden by vines that hung halfway over the opening. Mom ducked and started in. We followed like good Indiana Jones students.

"Whoa! This is scary," said Timmy.

"Just follow me. We're almost there," Mom announced. The cave grew darker, narrower, and damper by the second. My nose was stuffy from the mustiness of the cave. We came to a spot that opened up like a big room. Mom set down her lantern and called, "Tori, Timmy, come see this!"

"Oooo! Amazing!" I exclaimed.

There was a wild and amazing picture carved out of the stone, all different shapes that seemed to go together somehow, like a story. I would love to know who created it. At last I could relate to something my mom liked.

"This is called hieroglyphics. It's an ancient language spoken by the first people on the island. They tell a story. Chosen priests were the record keepers and had the responsibility to write the events of their time."

"Wow, how old are these?" I asked.

"They date back about two thousand years. When warrior tribes from Polynesia started moving in from the islands of the Pacific, the priests needed to hide and preserve their stories for future generations. They would etch these hieroglyphics in caves and caverns to do that."

There were six different circular etchings. They seemed to have different symbols in them. The

first one I saw had many circular lines carved in a pattern. In the middle there was a seven-pointed star holding a six-pointed star inside of it. I moved to the next circular drawing. It was an arrangement of triangles with a large triangle in the middle. There were other small symbols that were difficult to make out. I zoomed my eyes in on the smallest symbols.

"Mom, this looks like a flame from a fire," I said as I touched it. "And these look like running animals."

"Oh my gosh, Tori, you're right! I wonder...this seems to be telling a story of some sort of forest fire in that time. We had difficulty making out these small symbols. But, Tori, you're good at this!"

My eyes were drawn to the very last circular pattern. What? That looks like the compass! Exactly like the compass to the smallest detail! There was even a tornado coming out of it like the one I had drawn!

Is that Father North's compass?

CHAPTER 13

OPEN EARS

The next school day, Timmy and I walked home together as usual. We walked down the street and through the town park. We both were deep in thought and didn't say much until we reached our long, winding dirt road.

"Tori?" Timmy said. "I miss Dad."

"I know, Timmy. It's hard to go without him for so long. Just think, by your next birthday we'll be back with Dad."

"I know. But I feel like the big D is my fault," he said, never wanting to use the word "divorce."

"It's not your fault or my fault. It was an adult issue," I heard myself say, just like Father North had. "Mom and Dad love us both so much. They just couldn't live together anymore."

"We've only been here two months. I don't think I can do it without him for four more months."

Then I remembered my laptop at home. "Timmy, when we get home we can video chat with Dad. Would that help?" I asked.

"Why haven't we done that before?"

"I don't know. It's hard with the time change. Five hours is a big difference."

We picked up the pace and reached home quicker than usual. I got the laptop out of my yellow bag. We sat on my bed as we booted up the computer and clicked on Skype.

Ring! Ring! Ring! The screen turned on and we could see my dad's face!

"Well, well, well! What do we have here? Hey there, Sport! Hi, Angel!" Dad said.

"Hi Dad! We miss you. Especially me," said Timmy.

"I miss you, too. What have you been doing?" he asked.

"Tori took me to the beach with her friend and I went in the water!" Timmy said excitedly.

"Really?"

"Yeah, Dad, it was fun. My friends were surfing, and Timmy got his feet wet," I added.

"Well, I bet you guys didn't know this, but I used to surf when I lived in California."

"That is so sweet! If you can surf, I bet I could, too!" Timmy exclaimed.

"Not so fast, Timmy. You better learn to swim first!" Dad laughed. "What about you, Tori? What's been going on? Are you meeting some nice friends?"

"Things are okay. School is different. We had a Cultural Day, and we have an art fair coming up." Just then, I saw movement behind Dad's head on the video screen. "Is someone at your house right now?" I asked. "Ahh, why do you ask?" The movement happened again. But this time I got a better look. It was a woman! "I see her!" I yelled. "Who is there?"

"Tori, calm down. It's just a friend. Just like you are making new friends, so am I," he said as if it was normal.

"We have to go!" I said as I signed off and his face disappeared. I buried my face in my hands.

"Tori?" Timmy put his hand on my shoulder. "What's wrong? Why can't he have friends too?"

"Timmy, don't you get it? He is going to forget about us! He's not missing us. He's having fun with this new friend." Suddenly I could hear Father North's voice in my head: *Your parents tried patching the path for a while but have now learned that they need to pave a new path. You need to help others around you. Understand, you will all get through this.* Then I pulled Timmy close and we both cried. "I'm sorry, Timmy. It is okay for Dad to have new friends. Maybe she will help him get through this."

We heard Mom come in the door as she called, "Tori, Timmy, I'm taking you out to dinner. Are you here?"

"Okay, we're coming!" I yelled. "Timmy, don't tell Mom about the woman. We don't want her to be sad."

We went to Famous Pizza in town. It specialized in pizzas with Hawaiian flavor. The menu had coconut pizza, pineapple pizza, pork pizza, and seafood pizza. We sat in a booth near the back of the restaurant.

While we were looking at the menu, I couldn't help but hear the conversation at a table in the next row. A girl about my age was screaming at her little sister. "You brat! You can't do anything right!" Then she looked at her mom. "I'm so sick of this family! You don't care about me and what I want!" I had no idea what she was talking about. But all I could think was, is that what I sounded like? Did I talk like that to my mom and brother?

I decided that this must have been what Father North meant when he said "open your ears." I wasn't just hearing things around me; I was listening, too.

CHAPTER 14

MAKING CONNECTIONS

By the next week at school our art projects were done and getting matted by the art teacher. The mood was up. We were all excited about the art fair the following week.

One day after school, Lana caught up with me in the hall. "Tori, can you come over today? I know it's last minute, but I thought I'd ask anyway."

"This may be a good day! My mom is picking us up because Timmy has a dentist appointment."

We waited on the school steps until the little yellow car pulled up. Timmy ran ahead, but I caught up with him by the time he reached the car. "Mom! Lana wants me to come over. Can I, please?" I begged.

"That's fine, Tori. Do you have your phone?"

"Yes, I can call you later," I said.

"Okay. Call when they are getting ready for dinner and you can give me directions at that time."

"Thanks, Mom!" I said as I ran off to catch Lana.

James pulled up in his green SUV as he did every day. We climbed in. Lana sat in the front seat and I sat in the back. They lived close to the water like we lived close to the mountain. The house stood on stilts with the garage underneath. It was a pretty big house in comparison to the little shack we were living in. There was a big room when we went in the front door with a giant window that overlooked a bay. It felt light and airy like a tropical house should. Lana was lucky to have her own bedroom.

We went upstairs. Her brother's room had, of course, a surfing theme. There were surfboards hanging from the ceiling and a big wave painted on the wall.

Then we went into Lana's room. It was pink with tropical flowers dotting the walls. Her windows were decorated with leis and grass skirts. It looked like a hula-themed room.

"Cool room, Lana," I commented.

"Thanks! My mom is an interior decorator. She loves changing it all the time."

"When does she get home from work?" I asked.

"She makes her own hours, so she is here in time to make us dinner every night. My stepdad gets home about five."

"Stepdad? I didn't know your parents were divorced."

"They got divorced when I was five. Actually, James is my stepbrother," she explained.

"You're kidding! He is so nice. I never would have thought he was a stepbrother."

Lana laughed. "Why? Did you expect a stepbrother to be cruel like the mean ugly stepsisters in Cinderella?" I looked down and could feel her watching me.

"I don't know. My parents have only been divorced for a few months. So I'm still getting used to it."

"Don't worry. It gets easier. My dad is remarried also. Both of my parents are so much happier. Believe me, it's much more pleasant to be around them now."

"Really? Why did they get divorced?" I asked.

"I'm not sure of the real reason. They used to fight a lot. Sometimes they even got physical. They would throw things at each other. I remember hiding under the bed sometimes. My dad threw red soup on my mom's hair and it burned her. That was the last thing before they divorced. They don't fight like that anymore."

"My mom and dad would fight a lot, too. Not physical though. I'm a little weirded out with having them in two houses. Sometimes I feel like I'm stretching because they pull me to pick sides. And I feel like I have to lie so they don't get hurt feelings." It felt good to finally open up.

"Trust me, Tori, it will get better," she promised again. "Neither of my parents fight in their new marriages. It really is sort of fun to have two families. My dad has two babies with my stepmom. They're my half-sisters."

"I think my dad is dating someone. I saw her when we were on Skype. It made me mad!" I fumed.

"I was younger, but I would say you *want* him to find someone. He will be happier. Tori, you don't think your mom and dad would get back together, do you?"

I didn't want to admit I had secretly hoped that they would figure out they were making a mistake. But again, I heard Father North's voice in my head. They need to pave a new path. Now I understood. They were on the same path together but came to a fork in the road. They just chose to go two separate directions.

It was amazing how close I was feeling with Lana today. I guess I related to her in ways I couldn't relate to Bella at home. Bella didn't understand divorce because she had never lived through it. She was the one who always put the thought of "Maybe they will get back together!" in my head. Life was a fairytale to Bella.

When Lana's mom and stepdad came home, they invited me to stay for dinner. My mom spoke with Mrs. Lai on the phone to get directions to pick me up after dinner. It felt great to be with a family around the dinner table. They laughed and talked about their day. They did their "high-low" of the day. This was new to me. Each person around the table took a turn telling about what was the "high" of the day and "low" of the day. It came to my turn.

"My low of the day was when Kyle was teasing me at recess. But my high was coming over here and meeting such a great family. Thank you, Lana," I said.

Maybe it wouldn't be so bad after all. Lana's family seemed really happy.

CHAPTER 15

ART FAIR

The evening of the art fair quickly approached. Cars were packed in the parking lot and on the nearby grass like sardines in a can. All the families came to the art fair. It was an event that brought many community members as well. I had learned that Kauiaui Elementary was known on the island as the best fine arts elementary school because Mrs. Waters had won many awards for her students' artwork.

Mom and I walked in together. Poor Timmy had to miss it because he was sick at home with a fever. Mom had Gretta, from the dig site, babysit him. I felt bad he had to miss it, but I was kind of glad to have some time with Mom by myself.

We started in the gym, which didn't look like a gym at all. It was transformed into an art museum. There were paintings, drawings, and photographs hanging on temporary walls. Sculptures made of papier-mâché, clay, and plaster were scattered throughout. There were also mobiles hanging from the ceiling. Artwork was displayed from kindergarten kids all the way through fifth grade. Each piece of art had a typed paragraph next to it describing how the object changed the artist's history.

I led my mom up and down the aisles looking at all the projects. This is strange, I thought; mine is nowhere to be found.

We continued pressing through the crowd when I felt a jolt in my back. I turned around and Kyle's smile revealed his pearly whites. I had the most peculiar feeling as my heart skipped a beat. My mom winked at me with an all-knowing look as my face began to burn with embarrassment. I was suddenly short of breath.

Kyle kept walking. My mom looked at me and said, "So…it looks like you've made more friends than I thought! What's his name?"

"Mom, it's not what you think!"

"Oh, honey, I had my first crush in fifth grade, too." I kept walking. I did not want to talk about this!

We made our way to the main hall across from the principal's office. There, high on the wall, was my art project. The compass. People said it looked like a blown-up black and white photograph of a compass. The N had a curlicue on the end just like mine. The details of the different precious stones were at each cardinal direction. There was a purple swirl coming out of the center. A big blue ribbon was hanging from the top right corner of the matted drawing.

"Tori, that's beautiful! It looks just like the hieroglyphics we saw in the cavern. What a good memory you have!" She bent closer so she could read my paragraph.

A compass can change history. A compass can help one who is lost find his way. A compass can show a new way when a detour must be taken. My life has taken a detour. It was this compass that directed me onto a new path. It was this compass that helped me find my true north.

My mom looked at me with her eyes glistening, "Tori, I never knew you were such a talented artist. And you are such a deep thinker like your dad." With that, I also got tears and we hugged. "I'm sorry we made you take a detour," she added.

"Mom, I just want you and Daddy to be happy. I know it will take getting used to, but I understand this is for the best. Lana has two families now and they are all very happy." We hooked arms and began walking out the door. We skipped the school's ice cream social, but Mom took me out for ice cream instead. We sat together eating our favorite chocolate chip mint on a sugar cone. We laughed when we realized we both had the same ice cream mustache above our lips.

~

After the art fair, things got easier between Mom and me. The next couple of months seemed to fly by, and all of a sudden I realized I'd been here for five months already. I found myself spending more and more time at the dig with Mom when one day, as we were driving home, I said, "Mom, I want to show you something."

"Oh? Okay. Where?" she asked.

"Just park near the abandoned house. We'll walk from there."

Twenty minutes later, the car pulled up to the abandoned house. But it looked different. The steps had new wood on them where rotten boards had once been, and the hole in the door now had a new knob with a lock. What was going on? How was I going to get in the next time I needed to talk to Father North? Thoughts just kept shooting through my head.

"There's a new archaeologist starting to work next week. They're preparing this house to rent to him," my mom offered.

"Oh, really? When does he move in?" I asked.

"Saturday," she said with a smile. "It'll be a relief not to be the only house on the street, especially after you and Timmy leave. It will be too quiet."

I grabbed my bag, which contained the drawing pad and compass. "What I want to show you is this way," I said as I led her behind the house to the path

I frequently visited. We climbed in silence as birds and crickets chirped like flutes in a symphony. Geckos darted across our pathway. Finally the land started to flatten out and open up. There was the waterfall I had grown so fond of.

"This is fabulous, Tori. How did you find it?"

"I found this spot our first week here. This is where I liked to come and draw."

"I had no idea you could draw like you did for the art fair!" Mom said. "Your teachers have always said great things, but wow!"

"That's why I brought you here. I wanted to share my drawings with you." I led her up to the flat rock where I would sit at the base of the waterfall. We sat down and got comfortable. My drawing pad was nearly full now.

We opened up to the first page. It was a drawing of our first dog, Bailey. She looked so proud sitting there with almost a smile.

"You really captured her personality here. I know you loved Bailey," Mom said.

"She was a good dog. She would never hurt anyone. Then that careless driver had to come along," I added. The next page was a picture of our tree house we made with Dad. "Do you remember when we made this?" I asked.

"Do I remember? You were the best interior decorator around! That tree house looked like a penthouse dream vacation."

The third picture my mom studied was a portrait of her. Her hair was down and flowing with the wind. I could tell that she felt like she was looking in the mirror. "When did you draw this?" she asked.

"I've been working on it for a while. I wanted to remember the times when you were happiest. That is when you were sitting on a blanket at Island Park when we used to have picnics on Sundays," I explained.

Then she finally flipped through and came to the page I had been waiting for. Carefully studying the detailed compass drawing, she said, "What's this in the background? It almost looks like two windows." I could tell she noticed the hologram drawing of a figure behind the compass. "But they're actually big eyes, aren't they?" The two big eyes sparkled behind the compass and there were large hands beneath the compass.

"What is the story behind this?" she asked. "It's similar to the compass you drew for the art fair."

"When I saw the compass on the cave wall, it made me think. I thought about how a compass can guide you if you really pay attention. It almost talks to you if you listen. It keeps you on the Right Path. I

imagine this compass with a personality of its own."
My mom put her arm around me and smiled.

"I am so proud of you, Tori Jean. You are going to be very successful one day. Thank you for showing me this very special drawing journal. It makes me feel so good that you would share this with me," she said proudly.

We walked back to the car as the sun was sinking in the sky. The warmth in my pocket told me that Father North needed to see me. I said, "Mom, is it okay if I walk home from here? I'll be right behind you. I'm glad we had this time together, too."

"Sure. And Tori, we will make sure we have more time, just the two of us. This was so special," she said as she got in the car.

CHAPTER 16

THE AWAKENING

I knew I needed to see Father North. He hadn't shown up in a while, and I wondered if I was still on the Right Path. Was he gone for good? I had to find out.

I sat down on the newly constructed steps of the abandoned house and held the compass in my hand. The light of the full moon shimmered off the glass. I laid it down on the porch and waited for my friend and counselor. The swirl of purple smoke appeared, followed by the grand body of Father North in his white compass cape with his compass medallion. As he grew to his giant height, I watched in amazement as I did every time.

"My dearest, Tori. It has been quite some time since we have spoken. It appears that things are going quite well for you now," Father North began. "You have come a long way on the path you started on. When we first met, you were angry with the world and with your mother. This led you to make poor choices. Can you tell me anything you have learned along the way?"

"I think the biggest thing I learned is that the divorce was *not* my fault. I learned that my family is still a family even if it is split into two parts." I said. He took my hand in his big hand as he looked at me with the twinkle in his eyes I will never forget.

"Tori, dear child, you learned so much more than you realize. You opened your eyes and your ears. You opened your heart to your mom and your brother. This allowed you to stay on the Right Path and follow your true north. You must realize that you have your own internal compass. You are equipped to conquer the world! You just need to remember to listen to the voice inside your head and heart. Tori, you have one final mission. Your mission is to find another child who has lost their way. You must pass the compass on, but tell them nothing. It is their turn to find their true north," Father North explained.

"But...Father North," I choked. "I'm not sure I can do it without you!"

With that, he was gone. I took a big deep breath, picked up the compass, and slipped it into my pocket.

"I will find the perfect child to give it to," I promised myself and Father North. I knew he was still listening.

EPILOGUE

My promise to find a child "who has lost their way" was easier said than done. What did Father North mean? How was I supposed to know who had lost their way? I'd been keeping a lookout for the past month, but couldn't see anyone that looked lost.

Once again, I was flying across the world to go back to Michigan. Mom waved to Timmy and me as we went through the security checkpoint. She had a painted smile on her face, but I could see the tears in Mom's eyes, just as I felt the lump in my throat.

We were an hour and a half early, so we took our time walking to our gate. Most of the seats were filled in the lobby, so Timmy and I had to sit separately. Actually, I sat in a seat that was technically at another gate. I noticed the big sign above the flight attendant station that read ATHENS, GREECE.

I opened my drawing pad and began to people watch. It looked like many in the waiting area were going home, and I could overhear a foreign language, which I assumed was Greek. There were men and

103

women in business suits with briefcases, and other people in sundresses and sport clothes. There was a man sitting by himself with the bushiest eyebrows I'd ever seen peeking over the newspaper. I began to draw him.

I thought I heard a muffled cry. I looked around to see if Timmy was okay. He was fine and not crying. The crying continued which sounded like it could be a cat. After scanning the whole room, I looked under the chair next to me and saw a boy crunched up in a ball with his face in his shirt. He seemed my age! What was he doing?

"MAX! What are you doing, you good-for-nothing piece of trash!"

The airport lobby seemed to go silent. The older boy, who looked almost fourteen, laughed and said, "I'm just kidding, Max. Come out of there."

I could tell Max didn't think he was kidding. He slowly crept out from under the seats, leaving his backpack behind.

"Your dad wants me to watch you on this flight, so stay with me."

"Flight 129 to Athens, boarding section one," announced the flight attendant.

"Come on, Max, that's us!" said the older boy. Max followed him to the ticket taker and then looked up in a panic.

I knew I found who I was looking for! I grabbed his backpack from under the chair. In one fast motion, I reached into my pocket and grasped the compass. It felt warm as I slipped it into a small opening in the side of his backpack. Max quickly looked over his shoulder to see if the boy was still watching him and then took the backpack from me. We had a brief eye connection. When I looked into his dark brown eyes, he almost looked "lost." Although I had no idea what he was dealing with, I knew in my heart that I had found the right person. The warmth of the compass told me so.

Letter From the Author

Dear Reader,

It is my hope that you are able to identify with parts of my characters. The characters are fictional, however, I get many of my ideas from students I have had in my twenty-six years of teaching. As I have seen children of all ages struggle to overcome various challenges, I wanted to provide a non-threatening and entertaining way to counsel them. I wanted them to realize they are not alone. Children all over the world deal with issues such as divorce, bullying, handicaps, abuse, homelessness, alcoholism, and death. What I want you to walk away with is a feeling of knowing your "true north" and realizing that you have your own internal compass to help you find your way!

Sincerely,
Debbie K. Thomas

About the Author

Debbie K. Thomas was born in Kansas and raised in Michigan. She currently resides in southeast Michigan where she is an elementary school teacher. She has taught both special and general education students from Kindergarten through twelfth grade. The social issues that she has seen her students face are the inspiration for her books. Also, her desire to travel around the world brought her the idea for a series that visits all seven continents. Debbie is married to Craig and has two college-aged children, Dana and Kirk. *Keeper of the Compass: Secrets* is Debbie's first book. For more information and teacher resources, please visit Debbie's website, www.debbiekthomasbooks.com.

About the Illustrator

Aprylle Magar is a Michigan native who currently resides in Plymouth, Michigan with her husband, Av, and Bernese Mountain Dog, Maggie. She holds a bachelor's degree in Fine Art and Education from Eastern Michigan University. She teaches art to students of all ages. *Keeper of the Compass: Secrets* is the first book she has illustrated.